TOOT & PUDDLE

How Does Your Garden Grow?

For all the friends of Toot & Puddle,
new and old

All rights reserved. Published in the United States by Random House Children's Books,
a division of Penguin Random House LLC, New York.

Random House and the colophon are registered trademarks of Penguin Random House LLC.

Visit us on the Web! rhcbooks.com

Educators and librarians, for a variety of teaching tools,
visit us at RHTeachersLibrarians.com

Library of Congress Cataloging-in-Publication Data
Names: Hobbie, Holly, author.
Title: Toot & Puddle : how does your garden grow? / Holly Hobbie.
Other titles: How does your garden grow?
Description: First edition. | New York : Random House Children's Books, [2021] |
Audience: Ages 3–7. | Audience: Grades K–1. |
Summary: "Toot and Puddle are determined to figure out who keeps eating all the
vegetables in their garden every night." —Provided by publisher.
Identifiers: LCCN 2019050348 (print) | LCCN 2019050349 (ebook) |
ISBN 978-0-593-12466-6 (hardcover) | ISBN 978-0-593-12467-3 (lib. bdg.) |
ISBN 978-0-593-12468-0 (ebook)
Subjects: CYAC: Gardens—Fiction. | Pigs—Fiction.
Classification: LCC PZ7.H6517 Tob 2021 (print) | LCC PZ7.H6517 (ebook) | DDC [E]—dc23

MANUFACTURED IN CHINA
10 9 8 7 6 5 4 3 2 1
First Edition

TOOT & PUDDLE

How Does Your Garden Grow?

Holly Hobbie

Random House 🏠 New York

Toot and Puddle always planted their garden in May. This year Puddle's little cousin Opal came to Woodcock Pocket to help.

"I love gardens," she said. "Gardens are lovely."

They planted loads of lettuce. Toot planted spinach, squash, carrots, and peppers. Puddle planted beans and beets, plus pumpkins and popcorn. Last of all, Opal planted sunflowers and morning glories and crazy-colored zinnias.

Each morning they went out to see how everything in the garden was growing.

At the end of the day, they admired the garden in the evening light.

"It's beautiful," Opal said.

"I can't wait until we're picking things and eating them," said Toot.

"Well, we have to wait," Puddle said.

One morning Puddle noticed that some lettuce leaves had been nibbled up.

"Something likes our lettuce," he said.

"What could it be?" Opal asked.

"I think we have an uninvited visitor," said Puddle.

"We'll build a fence," Toot said decisively. "Gardens need fences."

The next day more lettuce leaves were missing.

"How did it get in?" Puddle wanted to know. "What can we do?"

"Catch it!" said Toot, who was absolutely furious. They hadn't tasted the lettuce themselves yet.

"Catch it?" Opal asked in a worried voice. "Maybe it won't come back," she suggested. Whatever *it* was. "Maybe it will just go away."

"Let's wait and see," Puddle said calmly.

The next morning there was less lettuce than ever.

Toot couldn't believe his eyes. "Outrageous," he fumed.

Opal said, "I think there's still enough for everyone."

The next morning . . .

"Holy moly," Puddle said. "Look at the spinach!"

"I don't believe it!" cried Toot.

"Maybe it doesn't understand," Opal suggested. Whatever *it* was. "Maybe it thinks eating things from our garden is okay."

So Puddle nailed a sign to the garden gate:

PRIVATE GARDEN. PLEASE DON'T EAT EVERYTHING.

Puddle couldn't sleep all night, thinking about the creature in the garden.

And Opal dreamed about who the creature might be.

The next morning almost all the bright-green leaves of new spinach were gone.

Toot said, "I'm going to stay up all night and catch whoever is devouring our garden."

"You can't do it alone," said Puddle.

The night was cool and bright. The three gardeners waited and watched for hours. At last . . .

"I think I see something coming," Toot whispered.

"Where?"

"There," Toot said. "From the woods."

Opal shivered. "Oh no," she muttered. "No, no, no."

"It's coming," Puddle said.

Whatever *it* was.

It took the longest time to reach the garden gate.

Very slowly, *it* climbed up the post and plopped—THUD!—into the garden.

They watched as it waddled through the rows of vegetables.

"It's eating our spinach," Puddle whispered.

"Attack!" Toot cried, and he raced for the garden, flourishing his hoe.

"Toot!" Puddle called after him. "Be careful! Don't hurt it."

Toot ran around the Vegetable Thief of Woodcock Pocket in a wide circle. "Stop that!" he shouted. "Away with you!"

"Yes, away with you!" Puddle cried, catching up with his friend.

Opal did not remain behind. "Excuse me," she called boldly. "Do you know you are in Toot and Puddle's garden?"

The creature just went on munching leaves of spinach, as though no one else were there. It made mumbling, grunting sounds of contentment.

"What can we do?" Puddle asked.

"You're under arrest!" Toot shouted. He waved his hoe in the air, but their unwanted visitor didn't seem to notice.

As dawn was breaking, the bulky, prickly intruder moseyed out of the garden, ambled across the yard, and disappeared into the woods.

"The fence won't keep him out," Puddle said.

"I don't think we can scare him away either," Toot admitted.

Opal was looking toward the dark woods. "I don't think he understands about gardens," she said.

For the next few days, the garden was not disturbed. Nothing came to eat the new green leaves of the carrots or the beets or the beans.

"I think it only likes lettuce and spinach," Opal said.

"Maybe you're right," said Puddle.

All week long, everything in the garden went on growing and blooming quite nicely.

But Opal had a feeling about the garden that wouldn't go away, and one evening at dinner, she piped up. "The garden is lovely," she said, "but . . . it isn't as exciting as it used to be."

"I know what you mean," Puddle said.

"Hmm . . . It really isn't," Toot agreed.

So the following morning, they planted another row of spinach right where the first row had been.

Puddle made a new sign, with Opal's help, and they hung it on the garden gate: